KU-685-292

 SCIENCE TIMELINES

THE AGE OF THE ATOM

1900 - 1946

By Charlie Samuels

W
FRANKLIN WATTS
LONDON•SYDNEY

First published in Great Britain in 2015 by
The Watts Publishing Group

Copyright © 2015 Brown Bear Books Ltd

All rights reserved.

For Brown Bear Books Ltd:
Editorial Director: Lindsey Lowe
Managing Editor: Tim Cooke
Children's Publisher: Anne O'Daly
Design Manager: David Poole
Designer: Kim Browne
Picture Manager: Sophie Mortimer
Production Director: Alastair Gourlay

Dewey no. 509

ISBN: 978 1 4451 4256 2

Printed in China

Franklin Watts
An imprint of
Hachette Children's Group
Part of the Watts Publishing Group
Carmelite House
50 Victoria Embankment
London EC4Y 0DZ

An Hachette UK company
www.hachette.co.uk

www.franklinwatts.co.uk

Picture Credits
Front Cover: Shutterstock

Inside: Corbis: Doug Wilson 31; **iStockphoto:** 14;
NASA: GRIN 5, 26, 29; Apollo Gallery 22, 23, 24;
Public Domain: Museum of Science, Boston 9; **Science
Photo Library:** Corning Inc/Emilio Segre Visual Archives/
American Institute of Physics 15; **Shutterstock:** Andrew
Bazylchik 18; Ferenc Cegledi 42; R Fonzales 30; Galaxy
Photo 33(t); Maram 44; Catalan Petolea 45; Richard Waters
39; **Thinkstock:** Brand X Pictures 7(t); comstock 10, 17;
istockphoto 8, 11, 13, 16, 33(b), 35, 41; Hemera 19, 38;
Photos.com 6, 7(b); Valueline 21; **Topfoto:** 37; PA 34.

Brown Bear Books has made every attempt to contact
the copyright holder. If you have any information please
contact licensing@brownbearbooks.co.uk

Contents

Introduction

The first half of the 20th century was dominated by two world wars. As always, conflict encouraged technological development as combatants raced to get an advantage.

The most promising area of scientific exploration was the nature of atoms, the particles that made them up and the power they contained. Nowhere did increased knowledge of the atomic and subatomic world have more profound effects than in electronics. The work of theoretical physicists such as Albert Einstein, who sought to understand the very nature of the universe itself, led to a practical appreciation of radio waves and the development of radio and TV. In transport, meanwhile, the coming of the aeroplane and the motor car were to be equally revolutionary. Not for the first time in history, scientific advances were changing the ways people communicated – and even how they thought.

The Influence of Warfare

In the shadow of the two world wars (1914–1918 and 1939–1945), weaponry became more powerful; an understanding of radio waves led to the technology of radar. Medical care advanced, too, with the creation of the first antibiotic, penicillin.

In the early 1940s, scientists in Britain and the United States experimented with unlocking the power of the atom. Just three years after they created the first controlled nuclear chain reaction in a room in Chicago, atom bombs were dropped on two cities in Japan.

About This Book

This book uses timelines to describe scientific and technological advances from about 1900 to about 1950. A continuous timeline of the period runs along the bottom of all the pages. Its entries are colour-coded to indicate the different fields of science to which they belong. Each chapter also has its own subject timeline, which runs vertically down the side of the page.

SAINT BENEDICT CATHOLIC VOLUNTARY ACADEMY

Radio spread rapidly through the 1920s and 1930s as a means of mass communication. It gave people more access to everything from sports to politics.

The Invention of Radio

Radio uses electromagnetic radiation, known as radio waves, which travel at the speed of light. It was called 'wireless', to distinguish it from telegraphs and telephones.

← Radios became common in many homes in Europe and the United States in the 1920s.

TIMELINE
1900–1902

KEY:

- Astronomy and Maths
- Biology and Medicine
- Chemistry and Physics
- Engineering and Invention

1900

1901

1900 Austrian neurologist Sigmund Freud publishes his seminal book *The Interpretation of Dreams*.

1900 Cuban-born US physiologist Aristides Agramonte y Simoni discovers that yellow fever is transmitted through the bite of a mosquito.

1901 Japanese-born US chemist Jokichi Takamine isolates epinephrine (adrenaline).

1900 German physicist Max Planck proposes the quantum theory: that radiation is emitted in separate 'packets', or quanta.

1900 The rigid airship LZ-1, designed by German engineer Graf Ferdinand von Zeppelin, makes its first flight.

1900 US inventor Thomas Edison invents the nickel–iron accumulator (Ni-Fe cell).

Radio dates from the late 19th century. Scottish physicist James Clerk Maxwell predicted mathematically the existence of electromagnetic radiation in 1864. He decided that light is just one part of the spectrum of electromagnetic radiation. In 1887, German physicist Heinrich Hertz discovered a new type of radiation: radio waves.

Using Radio Waves

In 1890, French physicist Édouard Branly devised the first way of detecting radio waves using a 'coherer', a sealed glass tube containing iron filings and an electrode at each end. When radio waves are present, the filings stick together and conduct electricity to form part of a circuit. English physicist Oliver Lodge improved it in 1894 and used it together with a spark transmitter to send Morse code messages a distance of 150 metres (490 feet). Russian physicist Aleksandr Popov conducted similar experiments a year later.

Unaware of these developments, Italian physicist Guglielmo Marconi also began experimenting with radio in 1894. In the process, he invented a radio antenna and the use of a ground (earth) with the apparatus. He could soon transmit coded messages over 3 kilometres (1.8 miles). The invention, known as radiotelegraphy, developed rapidly, especially after Marconi moved to

Timeline

1864 Radio waves predicted

1887 Discovery of radio waves

1890 Coherer for detecting radio waves

1894 Marconi's first radio transmissions

1903 Amplitude modulation (AM)

1904 Diode vacuum tube

1906 Triode vacuum tube

1933 Frequency modulation (FM)

↑ Some of the earliest radio transmissions used Morse code signals.

1901 English inventor Hubert Booth invents a vacuum cleaner powered by a petrol engine.

1901 German physicist Karl Ferdinand Braun invents the crystal detector for tuning a radio.

1902 French surgeon Alexis Carrel develops a technique for joining blood vessels end to end with fine sutures (stitches).

1902

1901 Italian physicist Guglielmo Marconi makes the first transatlantic radio transmission.

1902 French meteorologist Léon Teisserenc de Bort distinguishes the stratosphere and troposphere layers in Earth's atmosphere.

1902 German chemist Emil Fischer determines that proteins are polypeptides, made up from chains of amino acids.

Amplitude Modulation

Radiotelephony relies on modulation: altering a constant signal by a varying one. An audio-frequency signal from a microphone is amplified to vary an oscillator's radio-frequency signal, which is reamplified then transmitted. At the receiver, an antenna picks up the transmitted signal. It is amplified before being demodulated and amplified to reproduce the original audio signal in a loudspeaker.

→ Either the strength or frequency of the constant carrier wave can be modulated.

England in 1896. By 1901, he could transmit signals in Morse code across the Atlantic Ocean.

So far radio was an improvement on the telegraph because it did not need wires to transmit signals. But could radio be made to carry human voices, like the telephone? This question led to the development of radiotelephony, when Canadian-born US electrical engineer Reginald Fessenden invented modulation. Radiotelegraphy sends out pulses of short and long signals (the dots and dashes of Morse code). In radiotelephony, the transmitter sends out a continuous signal, a carrier wave, whose amplitude (strength) is varied (modulated) in step with the variations in the sound signals from a microphone. It allows the transmission of a range of sounds. Fessenden first demonstrated amplitude modulation (AM) in 1903. By 1906, he was able to transmit speech and music from a radio station in Massachusetts.

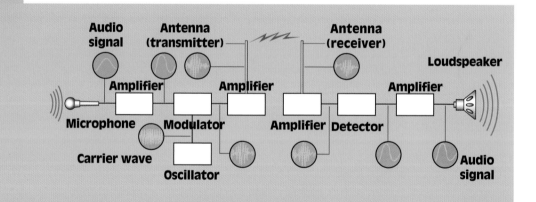

TIMELINE 1903–1904

KEY:

Astronomy and Maths

Biology and Medicine

Chemistry and Physics

Engineering and Invention

1903

1903 US brothers Orville and Wilbur Wright make the first sustained flight in a heavier-than-air aeroplane.

1903 German surgeon Georg Perthes first uses X-rays to treat cancerous tumours.

1903 Russian astrophysicist Konstantin Tsiolkovsky proposes the first practical theory of rocket propulsion.

1903 Dutch physiologist Willem Einthoven invents the electrocardiograph for recording electrical activity in the heart.

1903 Russian physiologist Ivan Pavlov develops the concept of the conditioned reflex (in which an action can be influenced by previous repetitive behaviour).

Improved Detectors

The new system needed a better detector. It came in the form of an improved crystal detector. The detector connected to the radio circuit by an adjustable thin wire, which soon earned it the nickname 'cat's whisker'. In 1917, Marconi began making VHF (very high frequency) transmissions. By 1924, Marconi was also sending speech signals from England to Australia using shortwave radio.

Radio receivers improved in 1912 when Fessenden devised the heterodyne circuit, which allowed more selective tuning. In 1933, American engineer Edwin Armstrong invented FM (frequency modulation). In this technique, the frequency (not the amplitude) of the transmitted carrier wave is modulated by the broadcast signal. As a result, transmission was less sensitive to static, producing an increase in the quality of the received sound.

↓ Marconi built a radio station in Ireland to transmit signals across the Atlantic.

↑ Italian Guglielmo Marconi developed radio into a reliable means of international communications.

1904 English physicist J.J. Thomson puts forward his model of the atom: a spherical mass of positively charged matter with electrons embedded in it.

1904 English engineer John Fleming invents the diode valve (vacuum tube).

1904

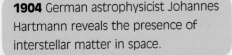

1904 German astrophysicist Johannes Hartmann reveals the presence of interstellar matter in space.

1904 The first section of the New York City subway opens, with electric trains serving 28 stations.

1904 English chemist Arthur Harden discovers coenzymes, molecules that are needed to trigger the action of enzymes.

The First Motor Cars

The car was the end result of a long effort to invent a motorised road vehicle. Early machines used a steam engine, the only motive power then available.

← A father and son show off their Model T Ford in the United States in the 1920s.

TIMELINE
1905–1907

KEY:

- Astronomy and Maths
- Biology and Medicine
- Chemistry and Physics
- Engineering and Invention

1905 German-born US physicist Albert Einstein publishes his special theory of relativity, one of the most important contributions in the history of science.

1905 French physicist Paul Langevin applies the electron theory to magnetic phenomena.

1906 French mathematician Maurice Fréchet introduces functional calculus.

1905

1906

1905 French psychologists devise a method of testing intelligence and ascribing an intelligence quotient (IQ).

1905 US engineer Almon Strowger perfects the dial telephone.

1906 English geologist Richard Oldham deduces that Earth's core is molten.

In 1770, French engineer Nicolas-Joseph Cugnot built a three-wheel gun carriage with a two-cylinder steam engine. Travelling at 5 kilometres (3 miles) per hour, it had the world's first motor accident when it demolished a wall. German engineer Charles Dietz built another three-wheel machine in 1835. It used a pair of rocking cylinders that moved a chain drive to the rear wheels.

Experiments with steam vehicles continued to produce a tractor or multi-passenger carriage rather than a personal vehicle. In England, William Murdock

Timeline

1770 Cugnot's second steam-powered gun carriage

1829 Steam-powered road vehicle

1865 Lightweight steam carriage

1885 Benz three-wheeler

1886 Daimler four-wheel car

1893 Benz four-wheel car

1896 First US automobile (Duryea) on sale

1908 Model T Ford

⬅ The very first cars had only three wheels, but engineers soon favoured the stability of four wheels. By the time of the Model T, tiller steering had been replaced by a steering wheel.

The first Benz car 1885

Panhard and Levassor 1894

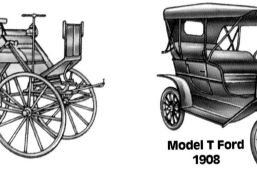

Daimler 1886

Model T Ford 1908

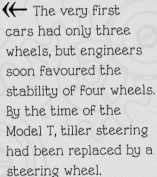

1906 New Zealand-born English physicist Ernest Rutherford deduces that alpha particles (produced by radium emission) are helium nuclei.

1907 Belgian-born US chemist Leo Baekeland invents Bakelite plastic.

1907 Swiss chemist Jacques Brandenburger prepares cellophane.

1907

1906 Austrian physician Clemens von Pirquet shows that hay fever is an allergic reaction to pollen and devises the term 'allergy'.

1907 US zoologist Ross Harrison begins the technique of in vitro tissue culture (growing tissues in glass laboratory apparatus).

1907 German chemist Emil Fischer confirms that proteins are made up of chains of amino acids by synthesising a polypeptide.

ran a model steam-powered road vehicle in 1784, and in 1789 US inventor Oliver Evans fitted a high-pressure engine to a four-wheel vehicle. In England, Richard Trevithick built a vehicle in 1801 with large wheels that reached 16 kilometres (10 miles) per hour. In 1829, English inventor Goldsworthy Gurney began a steam coach service, with an average speed of 24 kilometres (15 miles) per hour.

Around 1865, New Yorker Richard Dudgeon built a lightweight steam carriage, and in 1878 French engineer Amédée Bollée's carriage *La Mancelle* had a front-mounted engine. It could reach 40 kilometres (25 miles) per hour. However, just as they became efficient, steam carriages declined in the face of competition from the growing railways.

↑ By 1894, French motorists were organising speed and endurance races.

The Petrol Engine

The next step came from Germans Karl Benz and Gottlieb Daimler, who used the petrol engine. Benz's first three-wheel car dates from 1885. Its engine reached 13 kilometres (8 miles) per hour.

TIMELINE
1908–1909

KEY:

Astronomy and Maths

Biology and Medicine

Chemistry and Physics

Engineering and Invention

1908

1908 Danish astronomer Ejnar Hertzsprung introduces a method of classifying stars by plotting a graph of luminosity against temperature.

1908 The first Model T Ford comes off the assembly line in Detroit, Michigan.

1908 The Tunguska event occurs in Siberia; it may have been a comet colliding with Earth.

1908 US physicist William Coolidge uses tungsten to make an incandescent filament lamp.

1908 French anthropologist Marcellin Boule reconstructs the first complete Neanderthal skeleton.

1908 US inventor Elmer Sperry produces a gyroscope for ships.

Daimler built his first car in 1886, with a petrol engine in a heavier four-wheel vehicle. By 1891, French engineers René Panhard and Émile Levassor had front-mounted Daimler engines to drive rear wheels. They had modern steering, a gear box and a friction clutch. By 1893, Benz was making the more stable four-wheel cars with 2.24 kilowatt (3-horsepower) engines. The same year, US inventors Charles and Frank Duryea built the first petrol-engine car. The first US-made car (Duryea) went on sale in 1896.

Industrialist Henry Ford revolutionised car-making by introducing mass-production techniques at the start of the 20th century. As a chassis moved slowly along an assembly line, workers added different parts to it. In 1908, the method produced the Model T, or 'Tin Lizzy', as it was known. 'You can have it in any colour as long as it's black,' Ford was said to have said. The motor age was born.

→ The Model T had high axles to cope with rough, unsurfaced rural roads and tracks.

Henry Ford's Assembly Line

Henry Ford wanted to make the car available to all Americans by reducing the cost. He brought in an assembly system in which a chassis moved slowly along while workers repeated the same task on each chassis. A car could now be made in 1 hour 33 minutes, rather than the 12 hours it had taken before. Ford paid his workers high wages to keep his workforce stable. By 1914, one of Ford's own workers could buy a Model T with four months' pay.

1909 Danish chemist Søren Sørensen introduces the concept of pH, which measures hydrogen ion concentration to reveal the strength of an acid or alkali.

1909 French aviator Louis Blériot flies across the English Channel.

1909 Danish botanist Wilhelm Johannsen coins the term 'gene' for the factor that carries inheritable characteristics.

1909

1909 English physiologist Henry Dale discovers oxytocin, the hormone that controls the womb during childbirth.

1909 'SOS' is introduced as the international radio distress signal.

1909 Russian-born US chemist Phoebus Levene identifies the sugar ribose in some nucleic acids (now known as RNA, ribonucleic acid).

The Aeroplane

Even before the invention of flying machines, people wanted to imitate birds and take to the air. It was not until the 20th century that the ambition was realised.

→> The Wright Brothers' Flyer was a glider with an engine attached for power.

TIMELINE
1910–1912

KEY:

Astronomy and Maths

Biology and Medicine

Chemistry and Physics

Engineering and Invention

1910 New Zealand-born English physicist Ernest Rutherford proves the existence of the atom.

1910 French engineer Henri Fabre builds the first seaplane.

1911 Dutch physicist Heike Kamerlingh Onnes discovers superconductivity, the total loss of electrical resistance that some substances have at very low temperatures.

1910

1911

1910 US pathologist Francis Rous identifies the first cancer-causing virus.

1910 US airman Eugene Ely makes the first aeroplane flight off the deck of a ship.

1911 English physiologist Henry Dale identifies histamine, a substance released by the body to fight allergies.

The first heavier-than-air machines to fly were kites, invented by the Chinese around 1000 BCE. By the late 19th century, human-carrying kites were built. English soldier Baden Baden-Powell designed one in 1894, and American showman 'Colonel' Samuel Cody improved it in 1901. But real progress did not come until people began to experiment with gliders.

Off the Ground

The first person to build a steerable glider that could be controlled in flight was the German Otto Lilienthal. His first manned flight was made in 1891. His early machines copied birds' wings, but later he added a tail for stability and came up with the idea of two pairs of wings. The two-wing arrangement, later called a biplane, remained a feature of nearly all early flying machines. In the United States, Wilbur Wright and his brother Orville read about Lilienthal's pioneering work, which would influence their experiments. By 1903, they had perfected their human-carrying gliders.

Powered Flight

By the early 20th century, engineers had an 'airframe'. Now all they needed was a suitable power source. At the time, the steam engine was the only possibility.

Timeline

1808 Unmanned glider

1848 Steam-powered model aeroplane

1853 Human-carrying glider

1890 Unmanned steam-powered aeroplane

1891 Steerable human-carrying glider

1903 Sustained flight in petrol-engined aeroplane

➔ Otto Lilienthal makes his first glider flight in 1891. He later died in a glider crash.

1912 The largest extant lizard, the Komodo dragon, is discovered in Indonesia.

1912 Grand Central Station – the largest railway station in the world – is completed in New York.

1912

1911 German physicist Karl Ferdinand Braun devises a scanning system for cathode-ray tubes, later used for TV and radar.

1912 The RMS *Titanic* sinks on its first voyage, with the loss of 1,489 lives.

1912 German chemist Paul Ehrlich introduces acriflavine for use as an antiseptic.

The Wright *Flyer*

The Wright brothers' *Flyer* used a light aluminium petrol engine to power two 'pusher' propellers. The propellers rotated in opposite directions to keep torque from rotating the whole aeroplane. The pilot steered using a combination of the rudder and 'wing warping'. This involved flexing the ends of the wings (like a bird) to bank the plane into a turn. The pilot used the elevator to make it climb and descend. After several flights, with the brothers taking turns as pilot, the plane was damaged. It never flew again.

Various inventors tried their hands at flying steam-powered mono- and biplanes, but none succeeded in flying more than short distances before crashing. Steam engines were just too heavy for the task. The alternative was the petrol engine. In 1903, Samuel Langley built a full-sized aeroplane with a petrol engine. Two attempts failed – the machine crashing into Washington DC's

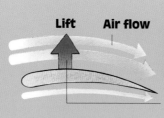

Lift   Air flow

The *Flyer*'s wings produced lift because of their shape. Air flowing over the top of the wing has farther to travel and moves faster than the air below. The faster air moves, the lower its pressure. This causes low pressure above the wing and high pressure below it, producing lift.

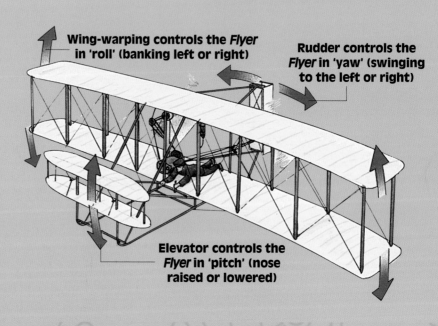

Wing-warping controls the *Flyer* in 'roll' (banking left or right)

Rudder controls the *Flyer* in 'yaw' (swinging to the left or right)

Elevator controls the *Flyer* in 'pitch' (nose raised or lowered)

TIMELINE
1913–1914

KEY:

1913

- Astronomy and Maths
- Biology and Medicine
- Chemistry and Physics
- Engineering and Invention

1913 US physicist William Coolidge invents the X-ray tube.

1913 US chemist William Burton patents a method for 'cracking' crude oil by breaking it down into simpler compounds using heat.

1913 US biochemists discover Vitamin A.

1913 French physicist Charles Fabry reveals the existence of the ozone layer in Earth's upper atmosphere.

1913 Danish physicist Niels Bohr proposes a model of the atom in which negatively charged electrons orbit a positively charged neutron.

Potomac River. The Wright brothers built their own petrol engine out of lightweight aluminium and attached it to one of their gliders. The launch of this machine at Kitty Hawk, North Carolina, on 17 December 1903 heralded the start of sustained heavier-than-air flight. For the first time, a human flew in a machine that took off and landed under full control. It was three years before another aeroplane succeeded – in 1906, Brazilian aviator Alberto Santos-Dumont made short flights in a motorised glider of his own design.

The next advances mainly involved materials. Steel and other alloys replaced wood for airframes, and aluminium panels instead of varnished cloth were used to cover them. Jets superseded petrol engines, and just 44 years after the Wright brothers' first flight, an aeroplane flew faster than the speed of sound.

↑ French aviator Louis Blériot's airplane lies on the ground near Dover, United Kingdom, after his flight from France in 1909 – the first long flight over a body of water.

1914 US psychologist John Watson proposes that experimental animals can be used to study human psychology.

1914 English military engineer Ernest Swinton proposes building the tank.

1914 German engineer Oskar Barnack produces a prototype Leica camera.

1914

1914 English astronomer Arthur Eddington recognises that nebulas are galaxies made up of millions of stars.

1914 The 64-kilometre (40-mile) Panama Canal is opened between the Atlantic and Pacific oceans.

1914 US inventor Garrett Morgan produces a practical gas mask.

Synthetic Drugs

The mid- to late 19th century saw chemists declare war on pain. Some developments came from traditional medicine, others came from experiments and a few were luck.

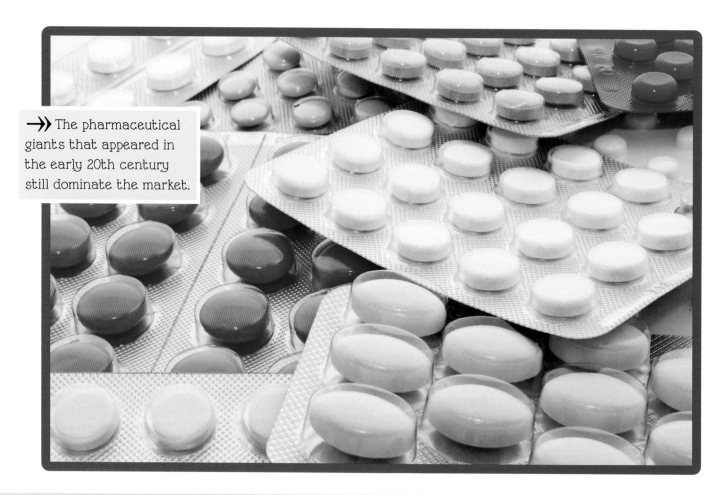

➤➤ The pharmaceutical giants that appeared in the early 20th century still dominate the market.

TIMELINE
1915–1917

KEY:

- Astronomy and Maths
- Biology and Medicine
- Chemistry and Physics
- Engineering and Invention

1915

1915 US astronomer Walter Adams identifies Sirius B as the first white dwarf star.

1915 English inventor William Mills invents the Mills bomb, a type of hand grenade used during World War I.

1915 The German company Junkers makes the first all-metal, cantilever-wing aeroplane, the Junkers J–1.

1915 US surgeon Alexis Carrel performs open-heart surgery on a dog.

1915 Bacteriologists independently discover viruses that attack bacteria.

1915 Scottish astronomer Robert Innes locates Proxima Centauri, the star nearest the Sun.

Humans have used naturally occurring substances as medicines for thousands of years. Some of them, such as opiates, were used as analgesics (painkillers) but they were never very reliable and they often had undesirable side effects.

The First Synthetic Drugs

The first totally synthetic drugs were gases. In 1799, English chemist Humphry Davy discovered the painkilling properties of nitrous oxide, also known as laughing gas. In 1815, similar properties were noted for ether vapour. But amazingly, it was another 30 years before medical practitioners were to take advantage of their painkilling properties to perform surgery. In 1847, a stronger anaesthetic gas, chloroform vapour, was developed by Scottish obstetrician James Simpson and used to help women during childbirth. None of the gases were free from side effects, however. They made the patient unconscious, or at least very woozy, and they were poisonous in large doses.

Timeline

1799 Nitrous oxide used as painkiller

1815 Ether used as painkiller

1828 Salicin isolated from willow

1847 Chloroform used in childbirth

1859 Salicylic acid in mass production

1899 Aspirin launched

1910 Salvarsan 606

← Before modern drugs, people relied on traditional cures or treatments made up and sold by herbalists. Some cures contained naturally occurring drugs that may have had real benefits – but many were useless and some were actually harmful.

1916 German-born US physicist Albert Einstein publishes his paper on the general theory of relativity, which mainly concerns gravity.

1917 The 2.5-metre (100-in) telescope is opened at Mount Wilson Observatory near Los Angeles.

1917 US nurse Margaret Sanger opens the first birth control clinic in the United States.

1916

1917

1916 Several scientists make special alloys.

1916 French physicist Paul Langevin produces a primitive form of sonar.

1917 The US Black and Decker company markets the first electric hand drill.

1917 English engineer Archibald Low invents an electronic control system for rockets.

The Wonder Drug

Aspirin is by far the world's most popular synthetic drug. About 100 billion tablets are used around the world every year. Aspirin forms the basis of many headache and cold cures; it is an anti-inflammatory and reduces fever. It may also help reduce the risk of heart attacks and prevent some kinds of cancer.

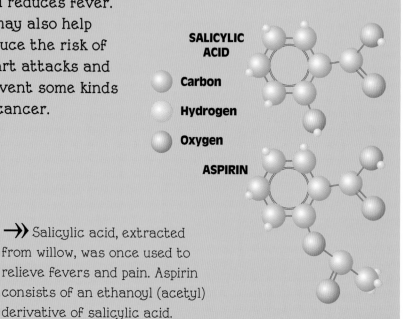

SALICYLIC ACID

Carbon

Hydrogen

Oxygen

ASPIRIN

➤➤ Salicylic acid, extracted from willow, was once used to relieve fevers and pain. Aspirin consists of an ethanoyl (acetyl) derivative of salicylic acid.

The use of certain plants to treat pain and fever has a long history. Ancient Egyptians used myrtle, ancient Greeks and medieval Europeans used willow and meadowsweet, and Native Americans used birch. All these plants contain the same active ingredient, called salicin after the scientific name for willow, *Salix*.

Wonderful Willow

The medicinal use of willow was rediscovered by English clergyman Edward Stone. In 1763, he reported that he had successfully used willow bark to reduce fever in 50 of his patients. The crucial breakthrough came in 1859, when a German chemist, Hermann Kolbe, worked out the chemical structure of salicylic acid and came up with a means of synthesising it on a large scale – not from plants but from coal tar. Using the Kolbe reaction, the new drug went into mass production.

Salicylic acid was an effective painkiller, but it caused stomach aches, so there was a need to modify the drug. The final steps were made

TIMELINE
1918–1919

KEY:

Astronomy and Maths

Biology and Medicine

Chemistry and Physics

Engineering and Invention

1918

1918 German physical chemist Walther Nernst puts forward a theory of chemical chain reactions.

1918 The world's most powerful radio transmitter begins operations at the naval station in New Brunswick, New Jersey.

1918 US chemist Winford Lewis develops the poison gas lewisite.

1918 US company Kelvinator markets the first mechanical refrigerator for home use.

1918 US embryologist Herbert Evans suggests that human body cells have 48 chromosomes each (in fact they have 46).

by German chemist Felix Hoffman at the chemical company Bayer. He adapted French chemist Charles Gerhardt's earlier formula to synthesise acetylsalicylic acid, and in 1899 the new drug was launched by Bayer as aspirin. At first, only doctors were allowed to administer aspirin, but in 1915 it became available without prescription.

Another drug developed at about the same time as aspirin was phenacetin. It later led to the development of acetaminophen as a painkiller.

Modern Drugs

The therapeutic advancements of the 20th century meant the science of pharmaceutics had finally come of age. The ability to synthesise new compounds and tinker with their structure to modify their pharmacological effects is the basis of almost all modern drug development and is continually undergoing further adaptations.

↓ Willow is just one natural source of salicin; the chemical occurs in plants discovered and used independently by ancient peoples around the world.

1919 US astronomer Edwin Hubble begins his long study of Cepheid variable stars in the Andromeda Galaxy.

1919 Austrian zoologist Karl von Frisch describes the 'dance' by which bees communicate with one another.

1919 US psychologist John Watson suggests that behavioural conditioning should be a subject of psychological research.

1919

1919 English physicist Francis Aston develops the mass spectroscope for separating isotopes.

1919 New Zealand-born English physicist Ernest Rutherford reports that he has disintegrated nitrogen atoms by bombarding them with alpha particles.

1919 British aviators John Alcock and Arthur Brown make the first non-stop flight across the Atlantic.

Subatomic Particles

By 1920, physicists knew every atom consists of a nucleus carrying a positive electromagnetic charge surrounded by a cloud of electrons carrying a negative charge.

 The paths of subatomic particles are traced through a cloud chamber.

TIMELINE
1920–1922

KEY:

- Astronomy and Maths
- Biology and Medicine
- Chemistry and Physics
- Engineering and Invention

1920 Scottish chemist Arthur Lapworth establishes the role played by electrons in organic chemical reactions.

1920 Ernest Rutherford predicts the existence of the neutron.

1920 US gunsmith John Thompson patents the Thompson submachine gun (Tommy gun).

1920

1921

1920 US astronomer Vesto Slipher detects a red shift in light from galaxies, showing that they are receding (and the universe is expanding).

1920 Station KDKA in Pittsburgh, Pennsylvania, begins the first regular radio broadcasts in the United States.

1921 English economist John Maynard Keynes publishes his *Treatise on Probability*.

E rnest Rutherford, the New Zealand-born English physicist, found that when he bombarded nitrogen atoms with alpha particles (helium nuclei), hydrogen nuclei were released. In 1920, Rutherford suggested the name 'proton' (from the Greek *protos,* meaning 'first') for the hydrogen nucleus.

Smashing Particles

Rutherford's research continued to centre on smashing atomic nuclei by bombarding them with alpha particles. In 1925, English physicist Patrick Blackett, working under him, developed the cloud chamber into a device for recording the disintegration of atoms. But alpha particles were not powerful enough to smash large nuclei, which repelled them without disintegrating. More energetic impacts were needed, and in 1932, English physicist John Cockcroft and Irish physicist Ernest Walton built the world's first particle accelerator at the Cavendish Laboratory in Cambridge.

Timeline

1920 Proton named

1925 Cloud chamber invented in 1911 developed further

1932 First antimatter particle, positron, discovered; neutron identified

1934 Neutrino identified and named

1937 Muon discovered

◀← Ernest Rutherford oversaw much of the early research into subatomic particles. However, the major breakthrough relied on the development of particle accelerators to create more powerful collisions between particles.

1921 Canadian physiologist Frederick Banting isolates insulin, the hormone that controls glucose levels in the blood.

1921 US airman John MacReady demonstrates spraying crops from an aeroplane.

1922 The BBC – British Broadcasting Company (later Corporation) – begins regular radio broadcasts in London.

1922

1921 The first motorway (Autobahn) opens in Germany.

1922 US anatomist Herbert Evans discovers Vitamin E.

1922 A Scottish team first use insulin to treat patients with diabetes.

1922 German chemist Hermann Staudinger recognises that substances such as rubber are natural polymers.

It used powerful electromagnets to fire accelerated protons at a target.

Nature of Radiation

In 1932, French physicists Irène and Frédéric Joliot-Curie found that alpha bombardment of paraffins or similar hydrocarbons (compounds of hydrogen and carbon) led to the emission of protons with very high energy. English physicist James Chadwick, working at the Cavendish Laboratory, conducted experiments which suggested that this high-energy radiation consisted of particles with approximately the same mass as the proton, but carrying no electromagnetic charge.

Chadwick thought the new particle was a proton bound to an electron (a hydrogen atom), and he was able to calculate the mass of the particle. Because it carries no charge, unlike an electron, the particle came to be called the 'neutron'.

↑ Scientists check part of the Large Hadron Collider, which shoots particles around a 27-kilometre (17-mile) underground loop in Switzerland.

TIMELINE
1923–1924

KEY:

	Astronomy and Maths
	Biology and Medicine
	Chemistry and Physics
	Engineering and Invention

1923

1923 Austrian doctor Sigmund Freud introduces his theory of the subconscious mind.

1923 Scottish engineer John Logie Baird invents a television system that uses mechanical scanning.

1923 Austro-Hungarian rocket scientist Hermann Oberth introduces the idea of escape velocity, the speed needed to leave Earth's gravity.

1923 US physical chemist Gilbert Lewis defines an acid as a substance that accepts electrons.

1923 US physicians George and Gladys Dick isolate the bacteria that cause scarlet fever.

1923 The German Benz company makes the first lorries with diesel engines.

In 1930, Wolfgang Pauli – one of the greatest physicists of the 20th century – was studying beta radiation, a stream of electrons emitted by unstable atoms. The electrons seemed to lose energy, but no explanation could be found for the loss. Pauli's solution was to propose that beta radiation also contains a previously unknown particle with the unusual properties of possessing no charge and no mass when it is at rest. The particle was later named the 'neutrino'.

During the late 1920s, theoretical physicists were very interested in the properties of electrons. American physicist Carl Anderson discovered the particle later called 'positron' in 1932, as did Patrick Blackett in 1933. It was the first antimatter particle to be identified.

→ Cockcroft and Walton's atom splitter was the world's first particle accelerator.

Building the Atom Splitter

In 1932, John Cockcroft and Ernest Walton charged a hollow metal chamber to 400,000 volts and injected protons into it. The positively charged particles were driven away from the high positive voltage along a series of tubes kept at lower voltages. They struck a piece of lithium. Alpha particles (helium nuclei) that were formed in the interaction caused flashes on an observation screen and were then photographed.

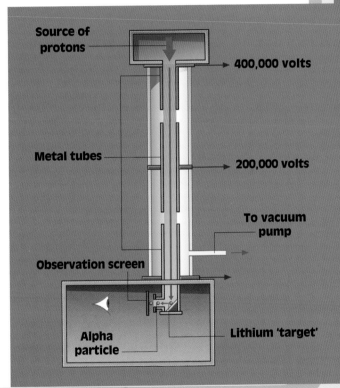

- Source of protons
- 400,000 volts
- Metal tubes
- 200,000 volts
- To vacuum pump
- Observation screen
- Alpha particle
- Lithium 'target'

1924 English watchmaker John Harwood patents a self-winding wristwatch.

1924 A team of US pilots makes the first round-the-world flight (they stop only to refuel).

1924 English physicist Edward Appleton uses radio waves to demonstrate the existence of the ionosphere, a layer of ionised gases in the upper atmosphere.

1924

1924 The Computing-Tabulating-Recording Company changes its name to International Business Machines (IBM).

1924 Swedish chemist Theodor Svedberg builds the ultracentrifuge.

1924 Australian anthropologist Raymond Dart discovers fossils of *Australopithecus* in Africa. They help establish Africa as the site of humanity's origins.

The First Television

In October 1925, Scottish electrical engineer John Logie Baird transmitted the first television pictures in his London workshop.

J.L. Baird, Early Television Transmitter.

← John Logie Baird produced this early portable television in 1949.

TIMELINE
1925–1927

KEY:

- Astronomy and Maths
- Biology and Medicine
- Chemistry and Physics
- Engineering and Invention

1925 English physicist Patrick Blackett begins experiments with colliding atoms in a cloud chamber.

1925 African American biologist Ernest Just shows that UV radiation can cause cancer.

1926 US physical chemist Gilbert Lewis coins the word 'photon' to describe a quantum, or particle, of light.

1925

1926

1925 US pathologist George Whipple discovers iron in red blood cells.

1925 US astronomer Edwin Hubble introduces a classification scheme for galaxies.

1926 US geneticist Hermann Muller produces genetic mutations in fruit flies by exposing them to radiation.

John Logie Baird was born in the west of Scotland and educated in Glasgow. His poor health cost him his job as an electrical engineer, and after three failed businesses, he retired to live in the southern English coastal town of Hastings in 1922. It was there that he began experimenting with television.

⬆ Baird poses with his early apparatus, including a Nipkov disk with a spiral of holes that scan an image as a series of lines as the disk rotates.

Capturing an Image

All television cameras require some method of scanning an image. Baird used a rapidly spinning Nipkov disc patented by Polish electrical engineer Paul Nipkov in 1884. It is a disc – Baird's was made from cardboard – pierced with a spiral of holes. As the disc rotates, an observer looking through it sees an object as a series of curved lines or scans, each of which is produced by a different hole in the disc. The first pictures of 1925 depicted a ventriloquist's doll named Stooky Bill. The first live subject (in 1926) was an office boy who worked in the premises below Baird's London workshop.

Timeline

1923 Zworykin invents iconoscope TV camera tube

1925 Baird's first television pictures

1929 BBC begins experimental TV broadcasts in Britain

1937 BBC begins commercial TV broadcasts

1938 Zworykin receives patent for iconoscope TV camera tube

1941 CBS in the United States begins experimental colour TV broadcasts

1926 Norwegian inventor Erik Rotheim invents the aerosol can.

1927 English zoologist Charles Elton publishes *Animal Ecology*, which establishes the science of ecology.

1927 English chemist Nevil Sidgwick introduces the modern theory of chemical valence, about the role of electrons in chemical bonds.

1927

1926 US inventor Robert Goddard successfully launches a liquid-fuel rocket.

1927 German theoretical physicist Werner Heisenberg formulates his uncertainty principle.

1927 US aviator Charles Lindbergh makes the first solo flight across the Atlantic Ocean.

The First TV Camera

The iconoscope was developed by Vladimir Zworykin in 1923 (patented 1938). An electron beam from an electron gun scans an image focused onto a photosensitive plate. Deflection plates make the electron beam scan in lines from side to side. Light striking the plate gives it a positive charge. Electrons not held by the charge bounce to another electrode and form the video signal.

⟫ Zworykin's iconoscope was the first successful television camera tube.

At first, Baird sent his television images along wires. By 1927, he transmitted pictures along a telephone line, and a year later he sent pictures over the Atlantic telegraph cable to New York.

In September 1929, the British Broadcasting Corporation (BBC) began experimental television broadcasts using Baird's mechanical system. The flickering images consisted of only 30 lines, later increased to 60 and eventually 240 lines. In 1932, Baird transmitted pictures by shortwave radio. The experimental broadcasts ended in 1935. By the time commercial television broadcasting started in Britain in 1937, the BBC had adopted the 405-line electronic system developed by the British company Marconi-EMI. But World War II stopped television broadcasting. Before the end of the war, Baird had produced colour television and three-dimensional images as well

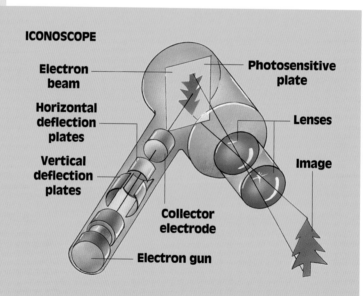

ICONOSCOPE

Electron beam
Horizontal deflection plates
Vertical deflection plates
Collector electrode
Electron gun
Photosensitive plate
Lenses
Image

TIMELINE
1928–1929

KEY:

- Astronomy and Maths
- Biology and Medicine
- Chemistry and Physics
- Engineering and Invention

1928

1928 US astronomer Henry Russell determines that hydrogen is the most abundant element in the sun's atmosphere.

1928 US mathematician John von Neumann outlines the foundations of game theory.

1928 US aviator Amelia Earhart becomes the first woman to fly the Atlantic.

1928 English theoretical physicist Paul Dirac predicts the existence of antimatter particles.

1928 Scottish bacteriologist Alexander Fleming discovers the antibiotic penicillin.

1928 US inventor Jacob Schick patents the electric razor.

as a widescreen system (by projection) and stereophonic sound. He died before television broadcasting resumed. When it started again, it used an all-electronic system.

Electronic Systems

Scottish engineer Alan Campbell-Swinton worked out the principles of an electronic system in 1908, although the apparatus was not available to put his ideas into practice. In the United States, Russian-born Vladimir Zworykin went the electronic route with his iconoscope. American inventor Philo Farnsworth developed a similar camera in 1927. Zworykin joined electronics company RCA and soon improved his system.

In 1941, the US company CBS made experimental colour broadcasts in New York, although regular transmissions in colour did not begin until 1951.

The Cathode Ray Tube

The cathode ray tube, invented in 1897 by German physicist Ferdinand Braun, was at the heart of TV receivers. Like the iconoscope, it has an electron gun and deflection plates and a coil to focus the electron beam onto the screen at the front. A phosphor, which gives off light when struck by electrons, coats the inside of the screen on which the scanned image builds up line by line.

← The screen of the cathode ray tube is coated with chemicals called phosphors.

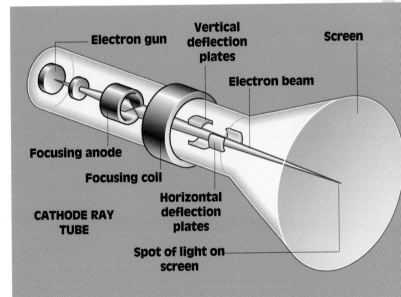

Electron gun
Vertical deflection plates
Screen
Electron beam
Focusing anode
Focusing coil
CATHODE RAY TUBE
Horizontal deflection plates
Spot of light on screen

1929 German biochemist Adolf Butenandt isolates the female sex hormone oestrogen.

1929 German-born US physicist Albert Einstein announces his unified field theory, which attempts to bring all the fundamental forces into a single theory.

1929 Japanese geophysicist Motonori Matuyama suggests that Earth's magnetic field has undergone reversals several times in its history.

1929

1929 German engineer Felix Wankel patents his rotary engine.

1929 A German Zeppelin airship makes a 21-day around-the-world flight.

1929 US astronomer Edwin Hubble formulates a law that relates the distance of a star to the speed with which it moves away from Earth.

Penicillin and Antibiotics

In the early part of the 20th century, millions of people died each year from bacterial infections. But the discovery of a mould that could kill germs would change all that.

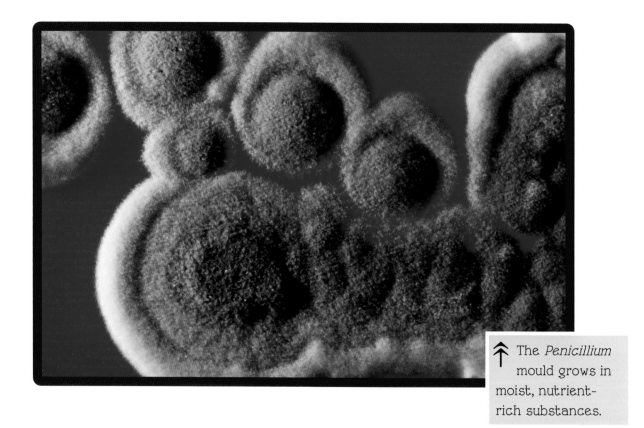

↑ The *Penicillium* mould grows in moist, nutrient-rich substances.

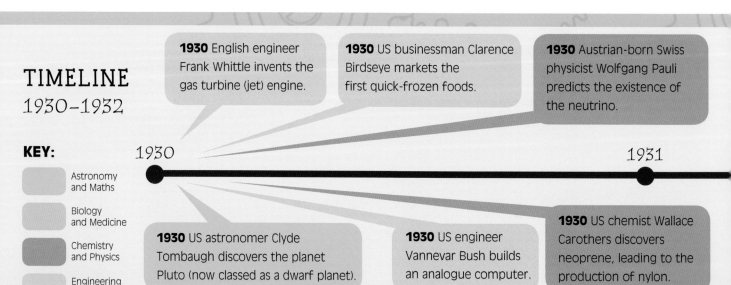

TIMELINE
1930–1932

KEY:

- Astronomy and Maths
- Biology and Medicine
- Chemistry and Physics
- Engineering and Invention

1930   1931

1930 English engineer Frank Whittle invents the gas turbine (jet) engine.

1930 US businessman Clarence Birdseye markets the first quick-frozen foods.

1930 Austrian-born Swiss physicist Wolfgang Pauli predicts the existence of the neutrino.

1930 US astronomer Clyde Tombaugh discovers the planet Pluto (now classed as a dwarf planet).

1930 US engineer Vannevar Bush builds an analogue computer.

1930 US chemist Wallace Carothers discovers neoprene, leading to the production of nylon.

From the late 19th century, thanks to the work of French chemist Louis Pasteur and others, scientists and medical practitioners recognised a new type of enemy – bacteria, or 'germs'. Many bacteria had been identified, and the conditions they caused in humans were better understood.

Discovery of Penicillin

Wound infection was the specialist area of Scottish bacteriologist Alexander Fleming. Unlike other medical researchers of the time, Fleming believed that the way to tackle infection was to harness natural processes to destroy infection through biological cures.

In 1928, after returning from holiday to his laboratory in London, Fleming noticed something unusual about a culture of *Staphylococcus* bacteria that he had left developing in a petri dish. In his absence, a mould had grown in the dish, and it appeared to be killing the *Staphylococcus*. Fleming identified the strange mould as a species of *Penicillium* and discovered that the liquid it produced (penicillin) was just as effective at destroying a large number of

↓ Alexander Fleming working in his laboratory at St. Mary's Hospital, London.

Timeline

1877 Pasteur observes anthrax-killing bacteria

1921 Fleming discovers lysozyme in living cells

1928 Fleming identifies penicillin

1940 Mice and humans treated with penicillin

c.1943 Penicillin in mass production

1931 US pathologist Ernest Goodpasture devises a way of growing viruses in chicken eggs.

1931 US chemist Linus Pauling explains the nature of benzene.

1932 British and Irish physicists carry out the first nuclear fission.

1932 US physicist Ernest Lawrence operates the first cyclotron, one of the first particle accelerators.

1932

1931 US radio engineer Karl Jansky accidentally discovers radio waves from space, leading to the science of radio astronomy.

1932 Synthetic rubber is first marketed in the United States under the name Duprene.

1932 The Sydney Harbour Bridge is completed in Australia.

What's in a Name?

'Antibiotic' means 'destroyer of life': antibiotics destroy the bacteria causing illness. In 1877, Louis Pasteur noticed that anthrax cultures died when mixed with other bacteria. In 1889, Frenchman Paul Vuillemin named the process by which one organism kills another 'antibiosis'. From that came the word 'antibiotic', first used by American biochemist Selman Waksman in 1941. He received a Nobel Prize in 1952 for his discovery of streptomycin, the first successful treatment for tuberculosis.

different bacteria. More exciting still, it appeared to have no effect on healthy living tissue, so Fleming thought it could be safe to use on humans. But there were drawbacks. For a start, there were several disease-causing bacteria – notably those responsible for plague and cholera – on which it had no effect at all. Even more disheartening was the fact that penicillin turned out to be very difficult to produce.

Fleming's work was followed up by an international team of scientists.

Manufacturing Penicillin

The problems seemed insurmountable at first, but in 1939, a group of scientists at Oxford University in England began following up Fleming's discovery. The team was led by Australian pathologist Howard Florey and German biochemist Ernst Chain. By 1940, they had extracted penicillin and began testing it on mice. A dose of penicillin enabled mice to fight off infections that

TIMELINE
1933–1934

KEY:

Astronomy and Maths

Biology and Medicine

Chemistry and Physics

Engineering and Invention

1933

1933 English engineer Alan Blumlein patents a system of stereophonic sound recording.

1933 The Boeing 247, the first modern airliner, goes into service.

1933 Polish and English chemists synthesise vitamin C, the first vitamin to be artificially produced.

1933 Swiss astrophysicist Fritz Zwicky suggests that space must contain invisible 'dark matter' (to explain the total mass of the universe).

1933 English aviator Alan Cobham devises a way of refuelling aeroplanes in flight.

1933 The Tasmanian tiger becomes extinct in the wild.

otherwise would have killed them. Thanks to refinements in the production technique developed by English biochemist Norman Heatley, the 'miracle' drug was being mass-produced in Britain and the United States by about 1943.

The development could not have come at a more crucial time. World War II was raging, and wounded servicemen were the first to benefit. Thousands of lives were saved, at least on the Allied forces' side. After the war, the benefits of penicillin were spread more widely. Fleming, Florey and Chain received the 1945 Nobel Prize for Medicine. Heatley was recognised by an honorary degree from Oxford University in 1990.

↓ Penicillin saved the lives of many wounded soldiers treated at field hospitals during World War II.

1934 Astrophysicists studying supernovas predict the existence of neutron stars.

1934 US scientist Royal Raymond Rife tests a cancer-curing treatment using radio waves.

1934 In France, Citroën launches the first mass-produced, front-wheel-drive car.

1934

1934 Dutch physicist Hendrik Casimir explains the phenomenon of superconductivity.

1934 English inventor Percy Shaw patents 'cats eyes', reflecting road markers.

1934 US psychologist B. F. Skinner invents the Skinner box for studying the psychology of animals.

The Development of Radar

During the 1920s and 1930s, researchers realised that radio reflection could provide a way of detecting planes and other objects, such as ships and icebergs.

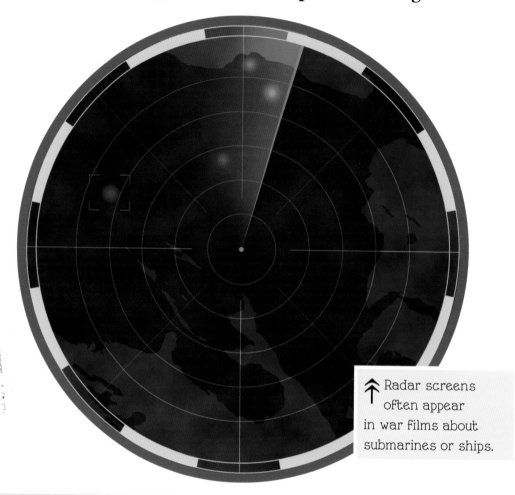

⬆ Radar screens often appear in war films about submarines or ships.

TIMELINE
1935–1937

KEY:

- Astronomy and Maths
- Biology and Medicine
- Chemistry and Physics
- Engineering and Invention

1935 US seismologist devises the Richter scale to measure earthquake intensity.

1935 Portuguese neurologist António de Egas Moniz introduces prefrontal lobotomy as a treatment for some personality disorders.

1936 Danish seismologist Inge Lehmann suggests that Earth's inner core is solid and surrounded by liquid metal.

1935   1936

1935 US amateur photographers invent Kodachrome transparency film.

1935 US chemist Robert Williams announces the structure of Vitamin B1.

1935 US physicist Arthur Dempster discovers the isotope uranium-235. It is later used in atom bombs.

In 1904, Christian Hülsmeyer patented a primitive radar system to warn ships of obstructions.

R adar stands for 'radio detecting and ranging', which explains exactly what the process does. To detect a plane, a radar set transmits a pulse of very high-frequency radio waves (microwaves), and a receiving antenna picks up any radio echoes that return. The direction of the returning signal reveals the direction of any target present. The range of the target can be calculated from the time it takes for the microwave signal to travel out and back.

The First Steps

In 1904, German engineer Christian Hülsmeyer took out the first patents for such a device. He planned a system that used continuous waves (not radio pulses) to warn ships of possible collisions. In 1922, engineers at the US Naval Research Laboratory in Washington, DC, sent radio signals across the Potomac River and detected passing ships when they interrupted the radio beam. In Britain, Scottish physicist Robert Watson-Watt was

Timeline

1904 Christian Hülsmeyer's patent

1921 Magnetron first invented

1922 US Naval Research Laboratory experiments

1935 Robert Watson-Watt's patent

1938 Klystron invented as an amplifier for radio signals

1939 Cavity magnetron

1939 Lawrence Hyland's demonstration

SAINT BENEDICT CATHOLIC VOLUNTARY ACADEMY DUFFIELD ROAD DERBY DE22 1JD

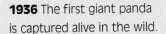

1936 The British Supermarine Spitfire fighter aeroplane makes its first flight.

1937 US electrical engineer George Stibitz makes a binary adding machine.

1937 The Golden Gate Bridge is completed in San Francisco in the United States.

1937 The Swiss company Nestlé begins selling instant coffee (Nescafé).

1937

1936 The first giant panda is captured alive in the wild.

1937 Swiss-born Italian pharmacologist Daniel Bovet identifies the first antihistamine substance that is effective in treating allergies.

1937 US physicist Chester Carlson invents xerography, a dry photocopying process.

The Cavity Magnetron

A cavity magnetron is at the heart of microwave devices, including radar. Inside a block of conductive material (the anode block) is a filament that generates electrons. The electrons are concentrated into a cloud by a magnetic field. As the cloud passes vanes inside the anode block, the electric charges generate a vibrating electromagnetic field. An antenna picks up the vibrations, which travel out through a waveguide as microwaves.

asked to investigate the use of radio beams as 'death rays' to attack enemy pilots. Using a BBC transmitter, he detected a Heyford bomber flying 11 kilometres (7 miles) away at a height of 3,000 metres (9,800 feet). By September 1938, with war approaching, the British built a chain of radar antennas on towers 100 metres (330 feet) high along the eastern and southern coastlines of England. They detected incoming aeroplanes at a range of up to 320 kilometres (200 miles).

Engineers also adapted radars to aim guns, particularly anti-aircraft guns and (in Germany) long-range naval guns. In the United States, Canadian-born engineer Lawrence Hyland renewed official interest in anti-aircraft and aircraft-detection radars, demonstrating a system on the USS *New York* in 1939.

Later Advances

The very high frequencies of radar signals require special electronics. Early transmitters used a

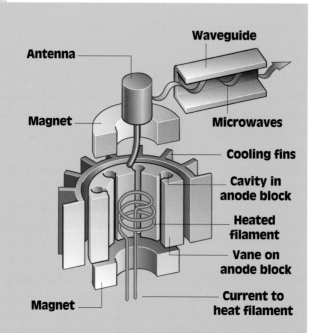

Antenna
Waveguide
Magnet
Microwaves
Cooling fins
Cavity in anode block
Heated filament
Vane on anode block
Current to heat filament
Magnet

TIMELINE
1938–1939

KEY:

- Astronomy and Maths
- Biology and Medicine
- Chemistry and Physics
- Engineering and Invention

1938

1938 The asteroid Hermes approaches closer to Earth than any previous observed asteroid: 780,000 km (485,000 miles).

1938 German physicists induce nuclear fission in uranium.

1938 German engineer Ferdinand Porsche designs the Volkswagen 'Beetle' car.

1938 US chemist Roy Plunkett synthesises the 'non-stick' plastic PTFE (Teflon).

1938 South African professor J. L. B. Smith identifies a coelacanth, a fish previously thought to be extinct.

1938 Hungarian-born Argentine inventor Laslo Biró makes a prototype of the first ballpoint pen.

vacuum tube called a magnetron. An improved version came in about 1934 from the French company CSF, invented by Henri Gutton. Two researchers at Birmingham University, John Randall and Henry Boot, developed a new device in 1939. It generated wavelengths as short as 9 centimetres (3.5 inches), and a radar using it could detect a submarine periscope 11 kilometres (7 miles) away. The British government immediately gave details of this 'cavity magnetron' (see box on page 36) to researchers in the United States.

After World War II, radar found a wide range of peacetime applications, such as air traffic control and ship navigation. In 1946, astronomers picked up radar signals reflected back from the Moon, and in 1958 from the planet Venus. The U.S. National Aeronautics and Space Administration (NASA) has used probes to map the bed of Earth's oceans and the surface of Venus. Weather forecasters use satellite radar, as do some law enforcement agencies to catch speeding motorists.

↓ Modern radar antennae sometimes resemble golf balls. This one guides aircraft towards an airport runway.

1939 US physicist John Atanasoff makes a prototype electronic binary calculator.

1939 US physicist Albert Einstein tells President F. D. Roosevelt that the discovery of nuclear chain reactions would lead to the building of bombs.

1939 US zoologist Victor Shelford introduces the concept of biomes (major geographical areas that support their own range of organisms).

1939

1939 French chemist Marguerite Perey discovers the radioactive element francium.

1939 The National Broadcasting Company (NBC) begins regular TV broadcasts in the United States.

1939 Swiss chemist Paul Müller realises the insect-killing properties of DDT (a synthetic chemical).

Rockets

The development of space rockets was led by Wernher von Braun. The German-trained engineer became a US citizen and worked on NASA's space programme.

➤➤ The V-2 rocket represented the pinnacle of von Braun's achievements.

TIMELINE
1940–1942

KEY:

Astronomy and Maths

Biology and Medicine

Chemistry and Physics

Engineering and Invention

1940 Three heavy radioactive elements are identified, including plutonium, by US physical chemist Glenn Seaborg.

1940 The Tacoma Narrows suspension bridge in Washington State collapses because of oscillation.

1941 German computer pioneer Konrad Zuse completes his third computer (the Z3).

1940

1941

1940 British and Australian scientists extract and purify penicillin and perform the first clinical trials of the drug.

1940 US zoologist Donald Griffin announces that bats 'echolocate' using ultrasound.

1941 Soviet nuclear physicists observe spontaneous nuclear fission in uranium.

As a boy, Wernher von Braun read science fiction by Jules Verne and H. G. Wells. He studied engineering at Berlin and Zurich universities. From 1930, he made experimental rockets for the German Society for Space Travel. Rocket testing was banned in Germany under the terms of the Versailles Treaty (signed in 1919 after World War I), so he worked on ballistics (missiles and bullets). The ballistics and munitions (weapons) branch of the German Army, led by rocket engineer Walter Dornberger, noticed his activities. Von Braun went to the newly established rocket research centre at Peenemünde on the Baltic Sea coast, where in 1936 he became director.

The Vengeance Weapon

At Peenemünde, von Braun's greatest achievement was the 'vengeance weapon' 2 (V-2). Originally designed by Dornberger in 1941 as the A-4, the huge rocket used liquid oxygen and alcohol as fuel, weighed over 11 tonnes, and delivered a warhead containing 1.1 tonnes of explosives. Its launch speed of 760 metres (2,500 feet) per second carried it high into the upper atmosphere, then it came down silently towards a target 320 kilometres (200 miles) away at over three times the speed of sound. Many of the V-2s launched

→ Wernher von Braun (arm in a cast) surrenders to the Americans in 1945.

Timeline

1936 Von Braun director of Peenemünde rocket centre

1942 Launch of first A-4 (later V-2) rocket

1946 Von Braun works at White Sands in the United States

1958 First US satellite

1962 John Glenn's orbital flight in Mercury capsule, *Friendship*

1969 *Apollo II* moon landing

1941 English chemists produce the plastic Dacron (Terylene), later licensed to US company DuPont.

1942 Italian-American physicist Enrico Fermi achieves the first controlled nuclear chain reaction, at the University of Chicago.

1942 German rocket engineer Wernher von Braun makes the V-1 and V-2 rockets.

1942 French diver Jacques Cousteau invents the aqualung, or scuba.

1942

1941 US biochemist Selman Waksman coins the term 'antibiotic' to describe new bacteria-killing drugs.

1942 US radio astronomer Grote Reber compiles the first radio map of the universe.

1942 The Manhattan Project, to make an atom bomb, begins in the United States.

Developing the V-2

The V-2 was the forerunner of all modern rockets. Von Braun based its development on papers written early in the 20th century by the US rocket pioneer Robert Goddard. Its engine was designed to fire for up to 65 seconds, to bring the rocket to the upper reaches of the atmosphere. At that stage, the engine cut out and the rocket angled itself to begin to fall towards its target.

→ Londoners clear wreckage left by one of nearly 1,400 V-2 raids on the British capital.

↑ An American soldier examines a partly built V-2 rocket at the end of World War II.

from 1944 fell on or around Antwerp, in Belgium, and on London. At the end of the war, von Braun chose to surrender to the US Army.

From 1946, he worked at White Sands Proving Ground, New Mexico, in the United States and in 1950 moved to the Ballistic Missile Agency at Huntsville, Alabama. There he adapted a V-2 to carry a nuclear warhead, creating the Redstone missile. Von Braun became an American citizen in 1955 and was recruited by the National Aeronautics and Space Administration (NASA). In 1958, he oversaw the successful launch of *Explorer 1*, the United States'

TIMELINE
1943–1944

KEY:
- Astronomy and Maths
- Biology and Medicine
- Chemistry and Physics
- Engineering and Invention

1943

1943 US scientists build the world's first operational nuclear reactor at Oak Ridge, Tennessee.

1943 Japanese physicist Sin-Itiro Tomonaga describes the basic physical principles of quantum electrodynamics.

1943 US company Dow Corning is set up to make silicone plastics.

1943 English mathematician Alan Turing oversees the building of Colossus, an electronic stored-program computer for breaking German codes.

1943 Dutch-born US physician Willem Kolff builds the first kidney dialysis machine.

1943 Austrian engineer Paul Eisler makes the first printed circuits for use in electronic devices.

A Controversial Figure

At the end of World War II, Werner von Braun and his team surrendered to the US Army. Von Braun later said that he wanted to make sure that knowledge of the weapon he had created would pass into the right hands. He and his team of technicians were secretly moved to the United States. Their past record of working for the Nazis was covered up. US authorities believed that rocket technology was more valuable than punishing the scientists for their role in the war.

The rockets displayed at the Kennedy Space Center in Florida are all based on Von Braun's basic designs.

first artificial satellite. He headed the team that built the Mercury capsules for the US crewed spaceflight programme. In 1960, he became director of the Marshall Space Flight Center, developing the giant three-stage Saturn V rocket for NASA's Apollo missions. The climax came in 1969, when American astronauts landed on the Moon. Von Braun retired from NASA in 1972. He died in 1977.

1944 US workers at IBM complete the Harvard Mark I calculator.

1944 Russian-born US engineer Igor Sikorsky builds the VS-36A, which sets the design of the modern helicopter.

1944 US physicist Robert Dicke makes a radiometer for detecting microwave radiation.

1944

1944 US physical chemist Glenn Seaborg isolates the radioactive elements americium and curium.

1944 US chemist Robert Woodward leads the synthesis of the antimalarial drug quinine.

1944 US bacteriologist Oswald Avery shows that nearly all organisms have DNA as their hereditary material.

Nuclear Fission

In the early 20th century, physicists realised that bombarding atoms with subatomic particles could release huge amounts of energy in a process called nuclear fission.

⟶ The best-known use of nuclear fission was in the creation of the atom bomb.

TIMELINE
1945–1947

1945 US government scientists make and test an atom bomb.

1945 Soviet physicist Vladimir Veksler designs and builds a powerful particle accelerator, the synchrocyclotron.

1946 US computer engineers build ENIAC (Electronic Numerical Integrator and Computer), a fully electronic computer.

KEY:

- Astronomy and Maths
- Biology and Medicine
- Chemistry and Physics
- Engineering and Invention

1945

1946

1945 English crystallographer Dorothy Hodgkin uses X-ray crystallography to determine the structure of penicillin.

1945 Chinese-American biochemist Choh Hao Li isolates the human growth hormone somatotropin.

1946 US chemist Willard Libby begins work on radiocarbon dating, a chemical way to date old organic material.

In 1932, John Cockcroft and Ernest Walton experimented with high-energy protons in the particle accelerator at the Cavendish Laboratory in Cambridge, England. In Paris in 1934, Irène and Frédéric Joliot-Curie found that proton bombardment sometimes produced radioactive isotopes. Two years later, Enrico Fermi found neutrons were more effective than protons at smashing atoms.

↑ Danish scientist Niels Bohr explained the principles behind nuclear fission.

Splitting the Atom

In 1939, Otto Hahn and Fritz Strassmann identified the products of uranium bombardment. Hahn and Strassmann had demonstrated that the uranium nuclei had broken apart. 'Fission' had occurred.

The same year, Lise Meitner and her nephew Otto Frisch, working with Niels Bohr, explained this result. Hahn and Strassmann found that, as well as a large amount of energy,

Timeline

1932 Cockcroft and Walton particle accelerator tests

1934 Joliot-Curies produce radioactive isotopes

1936 Fermi uses neutrons to smash atoms

1939 Hahn and Strassmann identify products of uranium fission

1942 First nuclear reactor

1945 First atom bomb tested and dropped

1951 Nuclear reactor built to generate electricity

← Italian physicist Enrico Fermi designed the first working nuclear reactor, which became operational at Chicago University in the United States in 1942.

1946 English engineer Frederic Williams makes a computer memory using a cathode ray tube.

1947 Italian biologist Rita Levi-Montalcini finds nerve growth factor (NGF) in chick embryos.

1947 US architect Buckminster Fuller invents geodesic dome construction for large buildings.

1947

1946 US engineer Percy Spencer invents the microwave oven.

1947 US airman Charles 'Chuck' Yeager makes the first supersonic flight, in a Bell X-1 rocket-propelled aeroplane.

1947 US inventor Edwin Land demonstrates the Polaroid camera.

Uranium Fission

Fission occurs when an atomic nucleus breaks in two, with the release of two or three neutrons. It can be induced by firing neutrons or protons at a nucleus. Fission releases an amount of energy equal to the energy that bound the nucleus together. When a neutron strikes a 235U atom, the nucleus absorbs it, becoming 236U, which divides into two lighter nuclei with the release of neutrons. If the neutrons strike other 235U nuclei, they, too, undergo fission, setting up a chain reaction.

uranium fission released neutrons that may trigger fission in uranium nuclei, which creates the possibility of a chain reaction.

Exploiting the Power of Fission

At the start of World War II, Bohr and John Wheeler published a paper describing the fission process. Meanwhile, Francis Perrin showed a certain 'critical mass' of uranium is needed to sustain a chain reaction.

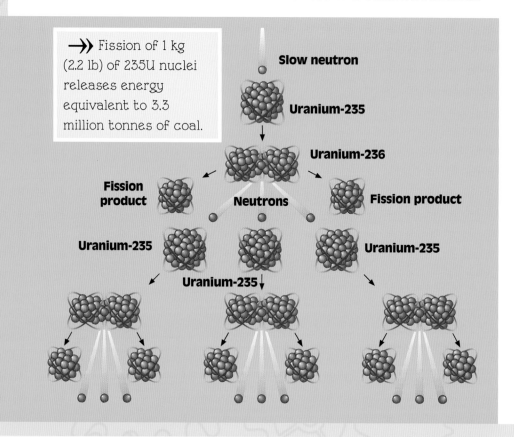

⟶ Fission of 1 kg (2.2 lb) of 235U nuclei releases energy equivalent to 3.3 million tonnes of coal.

Slow neutron

Uranium-235

Uranium-236

Fission product **Neutrons** **Fission product**

Uranium-235 **Uranium-235**

Uranium-235

TIMELINE
1948–1949

KEY:

Astronomy and Maths

Biology and Medicine

Chemistry and Physics

Engineering and Invention

1948

1948 US brothers Harold and Horace Babcock detect the Sun's magnetic field.

1948 US biochemists introduce the use of cortisone to treat rheumatoid arthritis.

1948 US physicists propose a big bang theory for the origin of the universe.

1948 US physicists Richard Feynman and Julian Schwinger independently formulate new versions of quantum electrodynamics.

1948 US electrical engineer Peter Goldmark invents the long-playing phonograph record.

1948 US musician Leo Fender and his colleagues market the first solid-body electric guitar.

Designed by Fermi, the first working reactor began operating in 1942 in Chicago in the United States. In 1951, the Experimental Breeder Reactor in Idaho became the first reactor to generate electricity.

It was clear that a sustained fission reaction could be used to create a bomb of immense power. Work to develop an atom bomb began in Britain and the United States. The two programmes were merged in August 1942 to form the Manhattan Project. The first successful test took place in the United States on 16 July, 1945. Atomic bombs were dropped on the Japanese cities of Hiroshima and Nagasaki in August 1945. The Japanese surrendered shortly afterwards.

⬆ Scientists watch a controlled chain reaction in the 'atomic pile' at the University of Chicago in 1942. Because of the radiation, no photographs could be taken, so the event was recorded by an artist.

1949 US microbiologists culture the virus that causes the disease poliomyelitis.

1949 US chemists produce the radioactive element berkelium by bombarding americium with alpha particles.

1949 US astronomer Frank Whipple suggest that comets are 'dirty snowballs', consisting mainly of ice and rocky debris.

1949

1949 English chemists use pulses of light in flash photolysis, for analysing ultrafast chemical reactions.

1949 US computer pioneers John Eckert and John Mauchly construct BINAC, a binary automatic computer.

1949 The first jet airliner, the de Havilland Comet, flies in England.

Glossary

alpha particle A helium nucleus emitted by some radioactive substances.

amplifier An electronic device that increases the strength of an input current or voltage.

anthrax A serious bacterial disease in animals that can also affect humans.

antibiotic A chemical that can destroy or inhibit the growth of bacteria or other microorganisms.

atom The smallest unit into which matter can be divided and still retain its chemical identity.

bacillus A cylindrical-shaped bacterium.

bacteria (singular bacterium) Microscopic organisms that can cause disease.

cathode The n or similar device, through which an electric current passes.

cathode ray A stream of electrons emitted by a cathode when heated.

DNA Deoxyribonucleic acid, the material that forms chromosomes that pass genetic information from parents to their offspring.

electron A negatively charged subatomic particle.

enzyme A large protein molecule that acts as a catalyst for the chemical reactions on which life depends.

geodesic dome A sphere formed from a network of triangular panels.

isotopes Forms of an element that contain the same number of protons but different numbers of neutrons.

lysozyme An enzyme that harms some bacteria.

Morse code An alphabet that uses long or short bursts of sound or light to create characters.

neutron An uncharged subatomic particle in the atomic nucleus.

nuclear reactor A device for generating electricity by nuclear fission or nuclear fusion.

nucleus The dense region at the centre of an atom, composed of protons and neutrons.

petri dish A shallow, circular, transparent dish used to grow microorganisms.

pharmaceutics The study of the creation of new medicinal drugs.

pharmacology The branch of medicine that studies the use and effects of drugs.

phonograph An early gramophone that could record as well as reproduce sound.

photon The basic particle of energy in which light and other electromagnetic radiation are emitted.

polymer A compound consisting of millions of similar links, used in plastics and resins.

proton A positively charged subatomic particle in the atomic nucleus.

radar An acronym for radio direction and ranging; a device that uses radio waves for detecting objects.

radioactivity The emission of particles or radiation by atomic nuclei.

seismologist A scientist who studies earthquakes.

stereophonic Using two sound channels that seem to come from different sources.

subatomic particle Any particle that is smaller than an atom.

supersonic Faster than the speed of sound.

torque A force that causes rotation.

vaccine A preparation containing viruses used to stimulate the body's formation of antibodies to build up immunity against infectious disease.

virus A tiny parasitic organism that can only reproduce inside the cell of its host.

Further Reading

Books

Car (Eyewitness). Dorling Kindersley, 2005.

Flight (Eyewitness). Dorling Kindersley, 2011.

Goldsmith, Mike. *John Logie Baird* (Scientists Who Made History). Wayland, 2003.

Holcroft, John. *The Story of Flight: A Three-Dimensional Expanding Pocket Guide*. Walker, 2014.

Mallam, John. *Guglielmo Marconi* (Great Scientists). Heinemann Library, 2009.

Middleton, Haydn. *Henry Ford* (True Lives). OUP Oxford, 2009.

Oxlade, Chris. *The Car* (Tales of Invention). Heinemann Library, 2011.

Parker, Steve. *Guglielmo Marconi* (Great Scientists). Chrysalis Children's Books, 2003.

Raum, Elizabeth. *The History of the Car* (Inventions that Changed the World). Heinemann Educational Books, 2007.

Spilsbury, Richard, and Louise Spilsbury. *The Television* (Tales of Invention). Raintree, 2011.

Tames, Richard. *Penicillin* (Turning Points in History). Heinemann Library, 2007.

Websites

firstflight.open.ac.uk/
Site with interactive history of flight.

inventors.about.com/od/ cstartinventions/a/Car_History.htm
About.com site on the history of the car, with links to inventors.

www.scienceclarified.com/ Mu-Oi/Nuclear-Fission.html
Science Clarified pages about nuclear fission.

www.autonews.com/files/euroauto/ inductees/history.htm
European Automotive Hall of Fame, with links to biographies of the many inventors of the first motor cars.

www.sciencemuseum.org.uk/ onlinestuff/stories/atomic_firsts.aspx
Pages from the Science Museum in London about atomic firsts.

Note to parents and teachers concerning websites: In the book every effort has been made by the Publishers to ensure that websites are suitable for children, that they are of the highest educational value, and that they contain no inappropriate or offensive material. However, because of the nature of the Internet, it is impossible to guarantee that the contents of these sites will not be altered. We advise that Internet access is supervised by a responsible adult.

Index

SAINT BENEDICT CATHOLIC
VOLUNTARY ACADEMY
DUFFIELD ROAD
DERBY
DE22 1JD